Omnibombulator was making his weary way along the lane as the light was fading, looking for somewhere safe to spend the night, when he saw a strange object under the hedge. It was an old boot, lying on its side.

Omnibombulator did not know what this huge thing was but he thought it looked a good place for a very small beetle to hide in . . .

OMNIBOMBULATOR

A YOUNG CORGI BOOK : 0 552 52799 8

First published in Great Britain by Doubleday
a division of Transworld Publishers

PRINTING HISTORY
Doubleday edition published 1995
Young Corgi edition published 1996

7 9 10 8

Set in Monotype Bembo Schoolbook by
Phoenix Typesetting, Ilkley, West Yorkshire

Young Corgi Books are published by Transworld Publishers,
61–63 Uxbridge Road, London W5 5SA,
a division of The Random House Group Ltd,
in Australia by Random House Australia (Pty) Ltd,
20 Alfred Street, Milsons Point, Sydney, NSW 2061, Australia,
in New Zealand by Random House New Zealand Ltd,
18 Poland Road, Glenfield, Auckland 10, New Zealand
and in South Africa by Random House (Pty) Ltd,
Endulini, 5a Jubilee Road, Parktown 2193, South Africa.

Printed and bound in Great Britain by
Cox & Wyman Ltd, Reading, Berkshire.

BULATOR

by
Dick King-Smith

Illustrated by
Jim and Peter Kavanagh

YOUNG CORGI BOOKS

Contents

Chapter One

The Naming

Omnibombulator was a very
small beetle.

He was born small, like all his
brothers and sisters, but unlike
them he stayed small.

Like them, he had six legs, but
his were very little legs and his
six feet were of a very small size.

One day his mother, June
Beetle, said to his father, whose
name was Bert, "Bert."

"Yes, June?" said Bert Beetle.

"What's the longest boy's
name you can think of?"

"Why?" said Bert.

"Because," said June Beetle, "we have one extremely small son and I think he should have a nice long name to make him feel important. So what's the longest one you know?"

Bert thought. After a bit he said,

OMNIBOM

"I've never heard of that before."

"You wouldn't have. I just made it up."

" 'Omnibombulator'," said
June Beetle. "I like it." And she
called her very small son and
told him his name.

13

"Do you think that's a nice name?" she said.

Omnibombulator scratched his very small head with one of his very small front legs.

"It's a bit long, Mum," he said in his very small voice.

"That's the whole point," said
his mother. "There's never been
a beetle with such a long name.
Now you'll be important and
everyone will take notice of
you."

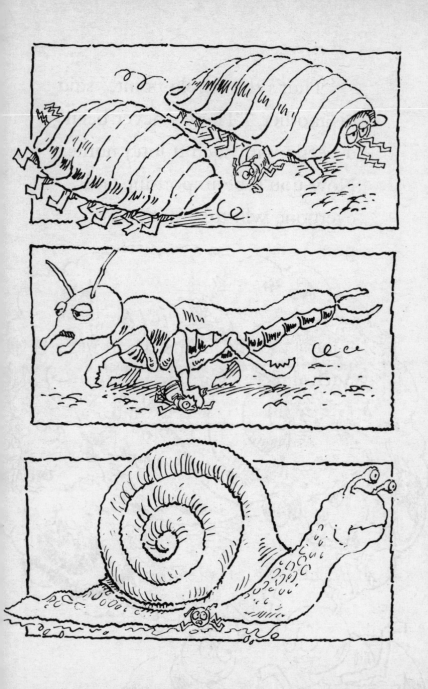

Chapter Two

The Big World

It didn't seem to Omnibombulator that his name made
much difference in fact.

Woodlice still pushed him out
of the way without so much as
a by-your-leave. Earwigs ran
over him as though he wasn't
there. Snails walked across him
and made him all slimy.

Even ladybirds tipped him upside
down and left him frantically
wiggling his six very small legs
in the air.

And, to his many brothers and
sisters, he remained extremely
unimportant.

"Out of the way, Titch," they would say as they scurried about the garden looking for food, that is if they bothered to notice him at all.

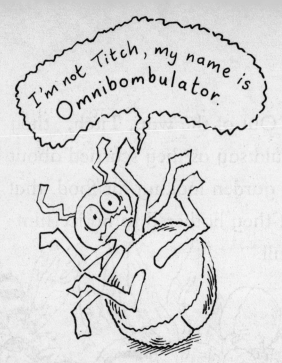

And when he said, "I'm not Titch, my name is Omnibombulator," none of them took a blind bit of notice.

Omnibombulator went, with very small steps, to find his father.

"Dad," he said.

"Yes, Omnibombulator, my
boy?" said Bert Beetle, rolling
the name round his tongue with
pride, for after all he had
invented it.

"Mum told me everyone
would take notice of me, but they
don't," said Omnibombulator.

"Maybe they don't see you," said his father. "After all, you are a bit on the small side. Try saying your name loudly when you meet someone. 'Hullo!' you must shout. 'My name is Omnibombulator!'

Once they hear that, it'll stop 'em dead in their tracks. What a name, they'll think! He must be a very important beetle!"

So Omnibombulator tried shouting his name at passers-by but, of course, it was a very small shout and most didn't hear him. The few that did said, "Omni what?" and then hurried away before he could say, ". . . bombulator".

Soon Omnibombulator began
to regret having been given such
a long name. Mum and Dad
were wrong, he said to himself.

It's not going to make me
important. I was better off when
I didn't have a name. And
anyway, I don't really mind
being small. It has its advantages.

And it did, because in the
garden there were not only
woodlice and earwigs and snails
and ladybirds, but birds too —

great monsters like blackbirds
and thrushes, that ate a lot of
the garden creatures, including a
great many of Omnibombulator's
brothers and sisters.

But because he was so small
and unimportant, the birds didn't
notice him.

So Omnibombulator gave up
shouting his name at passers-by
in his very small voice and
concentrated on staying alive.

As Omnibombulator grew up,
he became an orphan, for June
and Bert Beetle tragically met a
greedy bird one morning.

Omnibombulator could only be
glad that in their death they
were still together.

And now they're gone, he thought,
there's nothing to keep me here. I'll
set out to see the world and seek
my fortune. So off he set.

29

Chapter Three

The Journey

Because his six little legs were so
small, it took Omnibombulator
half a day to get out of the
garden and into a country lane.

I shan't see much of the world at this rate, he thought. Little did he know that soon he was to travel much faster!

He was making his weary
way along the lane as the light
was fading, looking for
somewhere safe to spend the
night, when he saw a strange
object under the hedge. It was
an old boot, lying on its side.

34

Omnibombulator did not
know what this huge thing was
but he thought it looked a good
place for a very small beetle to
hide in, so he plodded into it
and went to sleep.

Next morning he was rudely
awakened.

A whiskery tramp had been
trudging along the lane, after a
night spent under a haystack,
when he spied the old boot.

Now if there's one thing a tramp needs, it's a good pair of boots, and this tramp had a big hole in his left boot. The right boot was OK but the left one let in water all the time.

And this old boot, the tramp saw with pleasure, was a left one.

But would it fit? He sat down on the grass verge to try it on.

Omnibombulator was shaken violently out of a deep sleep as the tramp picked up the old boot and shoved his foot into it.

Hastily Omnibombulator
retreated before the huge
advancing toes until he reached
the inside of the toecap and
could go no further. Desperately
he pressed himself against its
leather wall.

Because the boot was a
fraction too big for the tramp's
foot, and because he was so very
small, Omnibombulator survived.

He was in total darkness,
jammed against a very dirty big
toe that stuck through a hole in
the tramp's sock, and the smell
was simply awful.

Now began a journey that was to take Omnibombulator far far away from his birthplace. The boot that had been his refuge was now his prison and might indeed have become his grave, because the tramp very seldom took his boots off.

Omnibombulator became faint with hunger, gassed by the smell of foot, and shaken half to death by the thump thump thumping as the tramp tramped along.

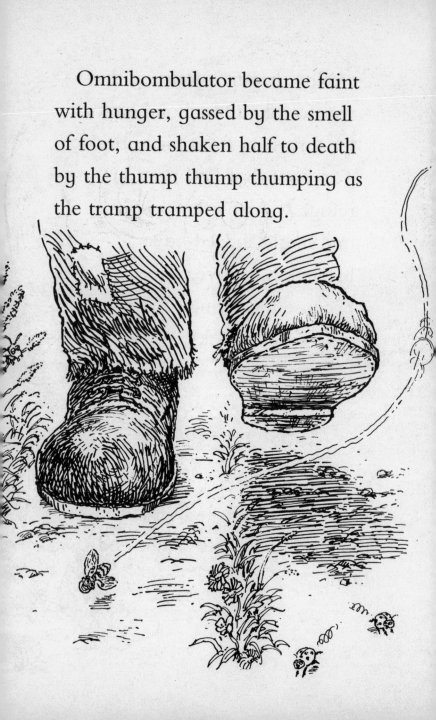

It's the end for me, he
thought. Soon I shall be once
more reunited with Mum and
Dad.

But just then the terrible
thumping stopped and the
horrible foot was withdrawn
from the boot. With the last of
his strength Omnibombulator
crawled out and wobbled away

from the tramp, who was sitting
by a river bank, dabbling his hot
feet in the cool water. Finally,
Omnibombulator was safe again.

Chapter Four

The Homecoming

Once Omnibombulator's very
small head had cleared and he
had filled his very small stomach,
he set out again on his six very
small legs.

The world, he decided, was
much too dangerous a place,
and he determined to return to
the garden of his birth.

The walk which had taken
the tramp a couple of hours took
Omnibombulator a week, but at
last he reached his goal.

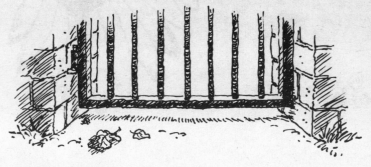

I may be small, he thought,
and I may be unimportant, but
I'm safely home at last.

But even as he was making
his way up the garden path, he
heard the beating of great wings.

He raised his very small head to see the most enormous black-and-white bird swooping down towards him.

As fast as his very small feet could carry him, Omni-bombulator made for a crack between the paving-stones.

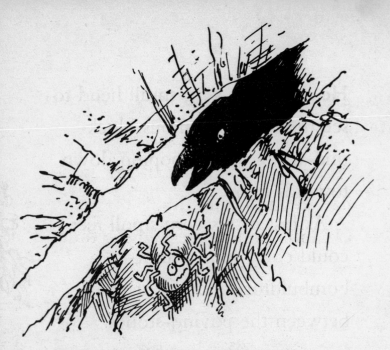

A very small crack it was –
much too small for any of his
brothers or sisters or his late
lamented mother and father to
have squeezed into. But Omnibombulator got down it all
right, just as the magpie landed
on the path.

It was pitch dark in the crack
between the stones as the bird
crouched above, but at last it
flew away again and
Omnibombulator could see that
he was not alone.

Another beetle was hiding
there too – a very small beetle,
exactly the same size as himself.
It must be a baby, he thought.

"Don't be scared, baby," he said. "I'm going to take care of you."

"MY!" said the other very small beetle. "You're a fast worker! We haven't even been introduced."

Omnibombulator could tell by its voice that it was a she-beetle.

He climbed up out of the crack and she followed.

"You're a little girl," he said.

"And you're a little boy," said she.

"Well, yes, I'm not big," said Omnibombulator. "I'll admit that. But you see, in fact, I'm a grown-up beetle. It's just that I didn't grow up very far."

"That's lovely!" cried the she-beetle. "Because that's just what happened to me. I'm a grown-up too! I'm just very small, like you."

How wonderful, thought Omnibombulator. We were made for each other.

"What's your name?" he said.

"I haven't got one," said the
very small she-beetle in her very
small voice. "They never
bothered to call me anything.
What's yours?"

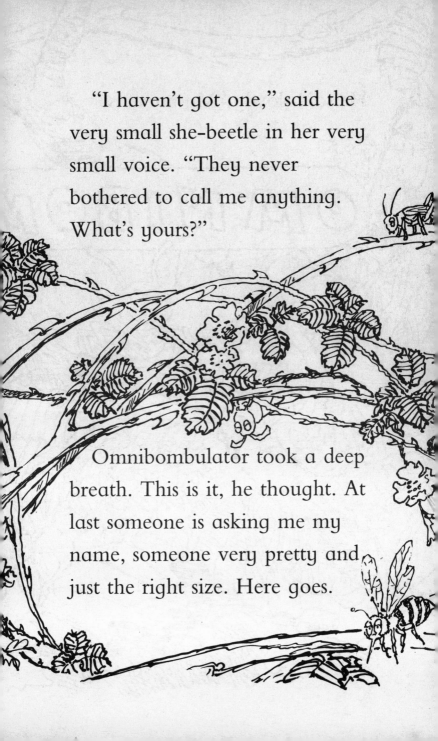

Omnibombulator took a deep
breath. This is it, he thought. At
last someone is asking me my
name, someone very pretty and
just the right size. Here goes.

He said slowly, "My name is,"

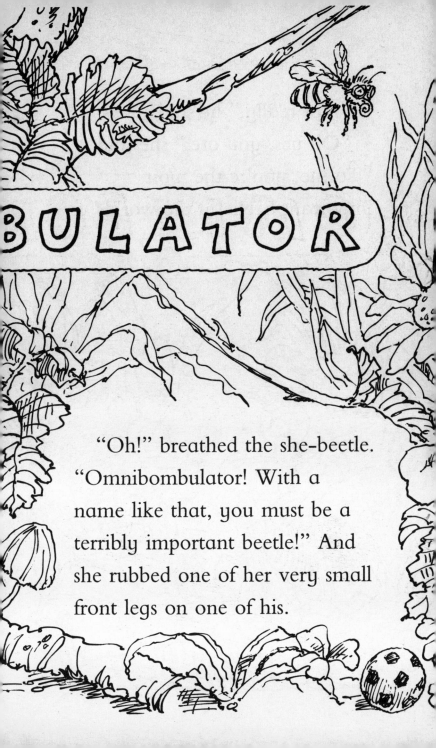

BULATOR

"Oh!" breathed the she-beetle.
"Omnibombulator! With a
name like that, you must be a
terribly important beetle!" And
she rubbed one of her very small
front legs on one of his.

"Not really," he said.

"Oh yes, you are," she said.
"To me, you're the most
important beetle in the world."

The End

Titles available by award–winning author
DICK KING–SMITH

Published by Corgi Pups
- **Happy Mouseday**★

Published by Young Corgi
- **All Because of Jackson**★
- **Connie and Rollo**
- **E.S.P.**
- **The Guard Dog**★
- **Horse Pie**
- **Omnibombulator**
- **The Dick King-Smith Collection**
  (includes **E.S.P., The Guard Dog** and **Horse Pie)**

Published by Doubleday/Corgi Yearling
- **A Mouse Called Wolf**
- **Harriet's Hare**
- **Mr Ape**

Published by Corgi
- **The Crowstarver**
- **Godhanger**

Published by Corgi (Poetry)
- **Dirty Gertie Mackintosh** illustrated by Ros Asquith

★ Also available in book and audio tape packs.

THE GUARD DOG
Dick King-Smith

*'Out of his hairy little mouth came the most
awful noise you can possibly imagine . . .'*

There are six puppies in the pet shop
window; five posh pedigree puppies, and a
scruffy little mongrel with a grand ambition
– to be a guard dog.

The other puppies laugh at him. How can
such a small, scruffy dog possibly expect to
be bought to guard a home? Especially when
his bark is the most horrible, earsplitting
racket they have ever heard! Will the poor
little guard dog be doomed to a lonely life in
the Dogs' Home – or worse . . . ?

0 552 527319

HORSE PIE
Dick King-Smith

Three magnificent horses – in terrible danger ...

Captain, Ladybird and Herbert – two Shire horses and a Suffolk Punch – are not pleased when Jenny, a retired seaside donkey, arrives at the Old Horses' Home. It's supposed to be a home for horses, and they don't want to share their field with a common little donkey.

Then rustlers are spotted in the area: thieves who like nothing better than to steal horses and ship them abroad – to be made into horse pie! Can Jenny and her friends save the huge heavy horses?

An exciting tale from Dick King-Smith, one of today's top children's authors.

0 552 527858